MW01487405

A
Place
Called
Heaven

LIGHTFALL
PUBLISHING

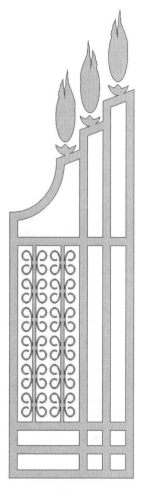

A
Place
Called
Heaven

Richard Sigmund

Foreword by
Dr. L.D. Kramer

ISBN 1-888398–18-3

DEDICATION

*This book is dedicated to the
many people who have encouraged
and supported this project.*

*Brother Greg
Carol Fraser, "On Eagle's Wings Ministry"
Dr. L. D. Kramer, "Challenge Ministries"
Robert Cesarek, "Love of God Ministries"*

*And the special words of
encouragement from,
Rex Humbard
W.V. Grant, Sr.
David Nunn*

Sigmund

Table of Contents

Foreword

Dr. Richard Sigmund, like Jeremiah the prophet of old, was called of God to be God's servant before he was born. Ever since he was a child, Richard has been used of God. He was known as "Little Richard" as a boy preacher and preached in some of the largest meetings in the world at that time: Oral Roberts, A.A. Allen, William Branham, Jack Coe, Kathryn Kuhlman and many, many more.

Brother Richard is a completed Jew, a man full of Faith and the Holy Spirit. Moving in the Gifts of the Spirit, the Gift working through him the most: Gifts of Healing. Richard Sigmund has one of the most miraculous ministries ever seen. So miraculous, in fact, that some of the miracles have truly staggered the imagination and stumbled the faith of many because they were so astounding. A few of them are recorded in his writing and tapes.

His testimony of his Death Experience and going to heaven is one of the greatest I have ever heard. I have met seven people who

9

have seen heaven and came back to tell of it, but <u>A Place Called Heaven</u> is the best I have ever heard.

I know that Dr. Sigmund's primary concern is to help the suffering to receive healing from the living Christ.

— Dr. L. D. Kramer, D.D., D.Min.

Preface

I can't explain it. I can only tell you what I saw. And language fails. It really is indescribable: the sights, the sounds, the sizes, the colors, the smells. How can one describe A Place Called Heaven?

I remember knowing things there that I can't remember now—or I am supposed to not remember. I was allowed to see many things and much more I was not allowed to see.

Many others have had similar experiences and some of the things were the same as what I saw. Others were not. And if you were shown A Place Called Heaven, you would see different things, too. Everybody who has an experience like this is going to see it differently. I can't explain it, I can only tell you what I saw. And I can only tell so much.

The things that I saw and I witnessed would probably not be the things that another person would see. We are each individuals and God deals with us in individual ways. The things that I saw relate to and ministered to me and will minister to those who read this book.

Besides, Jesus told me, "Don't ever forget how much I love you and what I have done for you. Never forget how much I love those that you are going back to and the place I have prepared for them and how much I love them."

I can't explain it, I can only tell you what I saw.

— Rev. Richard Sigmund

Introduction
Suddenly my body
was full of pain...

There was a sheet over my face.

Oh, did I hurt. But I sat up and said, "I ain't dead yet."

An attendant screamed. Another lost bladder control. Apparently, I had been dead for over eight hours and they were wheeling me down to the morgue. "He's been dead all these hours," I heard.

I could feel my bones knitting together. I could feel the scars healing while I sat up. And I breathed and spoke.

It was October 17, 1974, and I was coming back from Oral Roberts University (ORU). God had been speaking to me about the concept of blind, instant obedience—being broken like a wild horse is broken.

One reason I was at ORU was because of an

argument I was having with God. And there were several other issues in my life. I was having trouble with my wife in Arizona—big trouble. I was heading back to the church in Bartlesville.

But God had told me to go to ORU and tell Oral not to build the City of Faith: his big hospital. I didn't want to tell Oral that and kept avoiding contact. During the time, Oral kept looking at me, but I would not maintain eye contact. It was as if Oral knew I had a special word for him. But I left without telling him what God had told me to tell him.

I was driving a rather plush, luxury van. It even had one of those TVs that hung down from the roof. And if you moved it just right, you could actually see some of the program while driving.

Suddenly, without warning, I was in a thick, cloudy veil.

ONE
"You have an appointment with God"

All of a sudden I was in a veil.

It was like a thick cloud. There were gold, purple, and amber colors and a bright light. The cloud pulsated as sound was going through it. And I was going through it, too.

Behind me I could hear people talking. They were only a few inches away. There were sirens. Lots of noise. And I heard the words, "He's dead."

A force was drawing me through a glory cloud and on the other side of the cloud I could hear people singing. There was laughter with great joy and I was in total peace.

I could smell an aroma and a taste like strawberries and cream.

15

I was moving through the cloud and yet the cloud was moving through me. It took what seemed a few minutes. I then turned to the right to what appeared to be a receiving area.

Just a few feet from me, I could see two women standing. They were beautiful and of great age, but their countenance was as though they were in their mid-twenties. They were hugging each other and very joyous. And they were looking through the veil.

"He is coming. I see him. He is coming. Here he comes."

Suddenly, someone came through the veil. He had a profound look of confusion for a moment. He didn't know where he was. But just as suddenly he looked at the women and recognized them. They began to hug him and praise and worship God. It was a joyous reunion. You could tell.

Further to the right I noticed a group of about 50 people. They too were worshiping and praising God. They were standing there with their arms up just praising God. Some of them were just hugging each other and saying, "Here he comes. I see him coming."

They were apparently waiting for their pastor. Suddenly, he was in the veil. He had died.

As he appeared, he looked like a very old man. But as suddenly as he appeared into the heavenly atmosphere, all of the age lines in his face disappeared and his gnarled little body straightened up. This very old pastor looked in his mid to late twenties: his youth was renewed. He just stood there bewildered. But in a moment it dawned on him he was in heaven. He began to rejoice. And he began to say, "I want to see Jesus. Where is my Jesus. I want to see the Lord." People began to hug him and rejoice with him and he called them by name.

"Oh, it is you, brother, and it is you sister." He called them by name. And he said again, "I want to see Jesus."

Someone told him, "Oh, He is just a little further down your pathway. You will meet with Him. He is always there, right on time."

Then I noticed that there were angels there for him also. And angels for women who came through. And all up and down the veil, people were coming through. And there were always angels to meet them. As I understand it, no one has ever come to heaven without people to meet and greet them [except Abel].

Evidently, you can see into the veil from heaven but you can't see through the veil from earth. From our existence you can't see through the veil. And somehow you know when someone is coming through. People in heaven knew they should be at the receiving area when someone is coming. Later I learned there are announcement centers in heaven and people are notified that their loved ones were about to come to heaven.

The veil extended as far to the left and right as I could see. I had the impression it was hundreds of miles in each direction. And every few feet, there was a path leading into heaven. There was a path with the ladies. Everyone who came through the veil had a path unique for them. And I had a path— the path was for me.

Then I heard a voice: "You have an appointment with God"

Behind me, I could not see who it was, but I felt a familiar touch.

TWO
"You must walk on this path"

I must be in a place called heaven! What a wonderful, wonderful place.

I am standing on a golden pathway.

"You must walk on this path." The voice, gentle, yet firm, made it clear that I needed to be on this path. I wasn't about to argue with the voice.

The golden pathway was like a guided tour. It was a specific direction that I had to go. It would take me to things that I was supposed to see. It was about 6 feet wide— and had dimension to it—thickness. I was walking through a garden that stretched as far as I could see in either direction. And there were great groups of people.

On either side of the pathway was the richest turf-green grass I had ever seen.

And it was moving with life and energy. I knew that if I picked a blade of grass and then put it back down, it would just keep on growing. There is no death in heaven. Not even a blade of grass.

There were flowers of every imaginable size and color along the path. Some were the size of a dinner table. There were roses that were four feet across and had to weigh 50 pounds. Banks and banks of flowers. And as I walked, the flowers faced me. The air was filled with their aroma and they were all humming. I asked and was told I could pick one to smell. It was wonderful. When I put the flower down, it was immediately replanted and growing again. There is no death in heaven. It is against the law.

As I walked along the golden pathway, I saw the sky. It was rosette pinkish in color but still it was a crystal clear blue. Heaven was a planet—a very large planet.

And there were clouds in the sky. Clouds of glory. And when I looked more closely, the clouds were thousands of angels and thousands upon thousands of people walking in groups. They were strolling in the sky.

In the park there were benches you could sit on and talk to others. They were made of some type of solid gold shaped like wrought iron lawn furniture and they were everywhere. People were sitting and talking and praising God having a wonderful time talking with people who had just come through the veil. Others were there in great groups waiting for their loved ones to come through.

All the people were in preparation of loved ones coming into heaven. I heard someone say, "When he sees his mansion, he is going to shout glory."

Something just went all through me and I thought, "Maybe God has some place for me up here in heaven."

This beautifully manicured park was filled with huge, beautiful trees. They had to be at least 2000 feet tall. And many different varieties. Some I knew. Others, I had no idea what species they were. But tall and strong and no dead branches or limbs. Not even a dead leaf.

Some leaves were shaped like huge diamonds. Others were like hearts.

One tree that caught my attention was crystal clear. I was told it was a Diadem Tree. Each leaf was a tear-drop shape like a crystal chandelier. And there was a continual sound of chimes coming from the leaves as they brushed against each other in the gentle breeze—the beautiful sound of crystal. You could touch them and the sound would glow out.

But there was more. Each leaf, each limb, the entire tree gave off a tremendous glow with all the colors that were in the glory cloud. It glowed with sound and light. The tree was aflame with glory. The flame started in the root and went all the way through the branches out into the chandelier-like leaves. The tree exploded in a cloud of glory—a beautiful light. And it exploded with sound—an unbelievably beautiful sound.

The tree was huge. Miles and miles across. And glorious. Under it were tens of thousands of people worshiping; worshiping not the tree, but only God.

The further I went towards the Throne of God, the more trees I saw. Each was as glorious as the Diadem tree.

I came up to what I thought was a walnut tree. I was told to take and eat. The fruit was pear shaped and copper colored. When I picked it, another fruit instantly grew in its place.

When I touched the fruit to my lips, it evaporated and melted into the most delicious thing I had ever tasted. It was like honey, peach-juice, and pear juice. It was sweet but not sugary. My face was filled with the juice from the fruit. But nothing, by any means, can defile in heaven. Immediately, the beautiful sweet tree's fruit that touched my lips and its juice ran down my throat like honey. My face was just covered all over with this beautiful, wonderful liquid that this fruit turned into. Whatever it was, in that atmosphere of heaven, it was also instantly gone. It was a wonderful experience that I can still taste today.

There were also trees that had leaves that were shaped like hearts that gave off a beautiful aroma. I was told to take a leaf and smell it. I did. And a voice told me that it would give me strength to carry on. The moment I smelled the beautiful fragrance, I was strengthened.

23

I had this overpowering urge. I wanted to see Jesus. "Please, let me see Jesus."

THREE
"Behold the wall"

It was a mile away.

The angel walking with me pointed it out and said, "Behold the wall."

The wall was tall. Suddenly, I was at the wall. (Travel seems to be at the speed of thought.)

The angel said, "Behold the books."

On the left there was a book sitting on golden pillars: a giant easel. The book had to be a mile high and 3/4 mile wide. It was huge. And angels turned the pages of the book.

On the right was another book. It was the Lamb's Book of Life. The pages were turned and I was lifted up to see. There in three-inch golden letters outlined in crimson red was my name:
"Richard of the family of Sigmund: Servant

of God."

Along side my name was the date of my birth and the date of my conversion. The crimson red outline on my name was the sacrificed blood of Christ.

Revelation 21:27

Nothing impure will ever enter it, nor will anyone who does what is shameful or deceitful, but only those whose names are written in the Lamb's book of life. [NIV]

I went up to the wall. The wall was filled with all types of precious jewels: jasper, sardis, diamonds, yellowish/golden emeralds, bloodstone diamonds. The wall was made of some stone type material that gave off a sensation. When I touched the wall, it caressed my fingers.

I was told to go to the gate.

The gates were huge. 25 miles high. And there were three tongues of fire on each gate. The three flames represented the Father, the Son, and the Holy Spirit. The gates were made out of gold fashioned like wrought-iron—curved on the top, vertical stringers, and filigree between the stringers at the bottom. The gold represented the great mercy of God. Thousands of individual pathways came to the gate.

Through the gate along the pathway were many beautiful houses—mansions. And they had many verandas on the second, third, even the fourth floor. People would casually stroll off the edge of their verandas and very easily float to the ground. Or they would stay in the air. It seemed they could do either. The laws of physics don't seem to apply in heaven.

I was taken to a small lake and noticed that people were out in the water and even down below the surface of the water. The water was crystal clear and beautiful. It was even more clear than air is here. The people were down in it floating.

There is no death in heaven—it is against the law—so no one can die even though under water. Children can play in the water without fear of drowning. There are no dangerous water bugs or snakes. Nothing in heaven can harm you.

There were no waves on this lake. It was crystal clear and appeared to be miles deep: seemingly bottomless. It gave off a glow from the interior. I don't know what was down there, but it was glorious. Glory soil? Glowing rocks of jewels? But it—the water—was alive.

I did not get to go into the water, but I did put my hand in it. The water had texture to it. It would caress your hand. It was refreshing—like putting your hand in chilled 7-up. And it was still at room temperature—a glorious experience.

People could go down into it without fear. And I saw millions of people down in the water walking or floating hand-in-hand or even swimming. You could breath in the crystal-clear water. Coming out of the water, you were instantly dry.

At the Throne there are four rivers. The lake I was taken to was fed by one of the rivers. It was hundreds of yards wide and very deep in some places but shallow in others. As the river came out it began to multiply in amount.

The golden pathway led to buildings. Suddenly, I was there. The pathway stopped at a street made of some kind of clear substance. It was like a jewel. And the jewel was intermingled with strands of gold. The street was like a main street in a town. I was taken to a group of people. I noticed people watching my wonderment at the sights I saw.

And every little bit down the pathway, I would get a glimpse of Jesus just a bit further ahead. He was talking with people, loving them, hugging them. And they were looking at Him with such a look of adoration and worship. I wanted to be there just to fall at His feet, but the angel would say, "Just a little further on down the line. You have an appointment with God and you will meet with the Lord." It was boiling up within me. I just wanted to be with Jesus. But I knew I must wait.

In heaven everybody has his turn and nobody is anxious. I felt great tranquility because I knew that when it was my turn, it would be a glorious moment for all eternity. I would join with the others who in that moment of ecstasy got to see Jesus and talk with Him.

Though I could see Him ahead of me, I could not say He was not also right behind me. Jesus seemed to be everywhere at the same time. I just wanted to be with Him.

29

Sigmund

FOUR
"Would you like to hear me sing?"

A little girl came up to me.

She knew me. She was about eight years old and had beautiful blond hair. I knew she had died of cancer. And I think she was some kind of ambassador in heaven because all she did was go from group to group and sing glorious songs.

"Brother Richard. Do you want to see what I can do?"

She promptly proceeded to mess up her beautiful hair. Hair that she had lost when she suffered cancer. When she stopped, it immediately returned to perfection. There are no bad-hair days in heaven. And her hair was now beautiful.

"Brother Richard. Would you like to hear me sing?"

She started singing. The most beautiful, powerful, soprano voice you could imagine. Heaven's ambassador was singing and the choirs of heaven joined in. This was the most beautiful song I had ever heard—and she was only eight.

But she was not the only child I saw. There were many other children and each had abilities far greater than any adult on earth. If you could sing on earth, in heaven, you could sing a multiplied million times over. And this little girl had already exceeded anyone on earth.

No child is ever lost. Jesus has every one of them. And they are with Him. And they enjoy His presence. Many times I saw the Lord take little children and hug them and draw them to Himself and talk with them. It seemed so refreshing to Him that the little children were with Him.

In one place I saw a young boy sitting before a piano that must have been 100 feet in every direction. It looked like a baby grand piano, yet in the middle of it, there stood an upright harp. No one was playing it, but this young boy was sitting there and it was in an open place like a courtyard by some homes. As he sat there, he played the most beautiful music. It was a little bit like Bach, a little bit like Brahms, a little bit like Beethoven—it was amazing grace, how sweet the sound. Yet, now, I cannot tell you what the song was. When I left heaven, I left the song there.

But there was music and there were words to that song. And people joined in. While this child was playing the piano, the angels were standing at attention. Some with their arms raised worshiping God. This little child was playing this song with notes that were reverberating through all of heaven. Choirs were joining in. It was unbelievable. And glorious. And this little child was doing all of this.

I asked, "How can this be?"

One of the angels spoke to me and said, "They are playing this song because you are here. They want you to know that in heaven even a child can learn things that are impossible to learn while on earth."

I was told, "Look at the little child."

I noticed that he wasn't over 7 or 8 years old. He turned to me, smiled and waved his right hand and continued playing with his left. Then he stopped. The piano stopped. The harp stopped. The people stopped. Everyone started to smile and praise the Lord. The song was over, but I could somehow hear it echoing. The boy said, "I can play anything I want to." And everyone was happy about it.

I saw lots of children in heaven. Some looked like they had died during birth or shortly after. But in heaven they had total powers of speech and were completely sentient. They knew and understood what you were saying to them and could talk back—most amazing thing to see. I saw a number of children like this.

They were being carried by angels and by other people. There was a nursery in heaven where I saw hundreds, maybe millions of children of that age. They were tended to by angels and people who came by—and relatives, too. They grew up at a tremendous rate. They were not babies very long.

Then I saw children that were old enough to walk and run and play and they did just like they would play on earth. I saw one of the games they played. They formed a circle. There may be just a few or a lot of children in the circle. They picked someone and he would float in the air in the middle of the circle. Someone would give him a little shove and he would begin to float back and forth across the circle. They all giggled with great glee. The child floating through the air would giggle and giggle. It was a wonderful experience for them. It would be a great experience for me.

Another game was to see how far they could jump. Children would jump a hundred or two hundred feet in the air and float down like a butterfly: an amazing sight.

I didn't see anyone playing baseball, but I did see them climb tall trees and jump out of the trees and float down just like a little cotton ball. It was great excitement for them. No harm could come—they were in no possible danger.

I saw children playing along the shores of the seas and lakes. There are many lakes in heaven and there was no danger—no harm could come to them. They played in the water; on the water; under the water; swimming through the water or just sitting on the bottom of the lake. They were having a wonderful time playing with the rocks and building sand castles on the beach. What a wonderful childhood. Oh, to have been raised in heaven.

Then I saw as they grew older they began to attend school just like here on earth. But the schools were amazing. Children would learn things that geniuses here would not know or understand. I saw the Lord Himself come and take many children and hug them and squeeze them and tell them cute little stories. They loved Him and He loved them so very much.

I could not tell by looking at them if they had ever been sick. I am sure some had died here on earth and went to heaven, but when there, they were 100% absolutely healthy with rosy little cheeks—cherub-like—and they could run and play.

In one place I saw them having foot races. They would run faster than a horse could run. It was amazing.

Another place I saw them actually riding on some horses I saw in heaven. The horses loved it and they loved the children. The horses had the power of speech, the power of thought—it was a wonderful experience—they could talk. And there were other creatures in heaven.

It seemed mandatory that the children play and have a good time—that they be children. We know that on earth, if you don't have a very proper childhood, you won't have a proper adulthood. You can be wounded in your childhood and never emotionally mature in your adulthood. But in heaven, since everything is perfect, children have a perfect childhood. And they are welcome everywhere around everyone—everyone loves the children and the children love everybody.

I saw them playing what we might call "blind man's bluff." One would run and hide and they would find each other and then start the game all over. It was just a beautiful thing that I saw.

I was not allowed to talk with any of them except the girl who sang. At the time, there was a purpose. Now, I don't know what it was.

There was a beautiful children's choir. The children had singing and musical capabilities far beyond anything you could imagine on earth. Every child could sing. It was a truly heavenly choir. I was told that the talents and abilities that God ordained for them from birth are magnified millions of times over in heaven.

I saw a child about five years old sitting at an easel painting. He would tell the paint brush the color or colors he wanted and the paint brush would turn to that color. I saw him painting a picture of the country side and he would say, "No. Darker. The tree must be darker." The paint brush would turn that color and he would just wipe it across the canvas one time and the tree would appear. In heaven, all things are possible.

All of the children were very happy. For all the children, their hair was perfect, their clothing was perfect. Some had little play suits on. Some had robes. Others didn't.

All the children were very friendly and very loving. They called each other by their first name and they were called by their first name. They also called the angels by name. (I can't remember any of the names.) In heaven, everybody knows everybody and knows them by name. Heaven is a place you want to go. Just to be around the children, if nothing else.

FIVE
House of Pearl

J ust   before I was taken to the Throne, I saw one avenue just off the street I was walking on. It was a huge avenue that branched off a little bit to the right and joined with another main street that went down heaven. The avenue was 20 - 30 miles long and I could plainly see the other side. The avenue was about 250 feet wide and people were walking up and down the beautiful golden and crystal streets that were made of diamonds or maybe just one big diamond of some kind. You could see through this diamond and it had layers of gold and silver and there were precious stones everywhere. There were mansions on this street beyond compare. I was told they were for missionaries. Everything they gave, they gave to the Lord. I believe that in heaven God rewards everything that we can't receive here.

I do not know the names of those who lived down that street because I was not allowed to go there, but I know some of them were modern-day missionaries. Some had just recently died and there were large groups of people welcoming them at the veil. I saw one coming and he was dressed in a beautiful robe. One of the first things he did was grab his clothes and say, "Oh, how beautiful. I am not in rags anymore." His robe was spun gold. And there were thousands of people meeting him. The rewards of missionaries are great and God loves missionary-minded people.

I was taken to one house on the street I was walking. It was a single house carved out of a single, giant pearl. It was 250-300 feet across and 100 feet tall. It was a mansion carved out of a pearl.

The furniture in it was formed by angels who molded and carved the pearl into shape. Even the chandelier was carved out of the pearl and it was lit. It glowed from within.

The house made of pearl belonged to a woman and the angels told me her story.

Her name was Pearl and she was a missionary. She was known for her giving to the poor. Eventually, she died of starvation. The house of pearl was a reward for a pure heart.

There were many other houses on this street. Many different kinds. And they were unbelievable to even consider building any place but in heaven.

One street corner I was going by—whether walking or floating, I do not know, an angel was holding me by the arm—I wanted to stop and see a specific mansion. We stopped for a moment. It appeared to be made of solid gold but there was wood there, too. There were hundreds of people in this mansion. All were people that this one missionary had led to the Lord. He had been a part of their family's lives. Now they were still a part of his big family and they were really joyous. It was unbelievable the peace and tranquility that was there. As I walked by they yelled at me and said, "Hello, Richard. It is good to see you." And they waved. They knew me but I didn't seem to know any of them—or remember knowing them.

Everybody in heaven is so friendly. People would yell from across the street, "Hello Richard. How are you doing?"

And there were larger buildings on this street. Of all the buildings I saw, none of the doors had locks and the doors were not closed. Whether mansions, smaller homes, apartment buildings (yes, some people like living in condominiums), all were open. Some had windows, but some did not. There are no storms and there are no thieves. Everyone who comes is perfectly welcome to come into your house whether you are there or not. But I believe out of respect, I don't think anyone enters into anyone else's home when the owner is not there.

I saw houses that were brightly lit from the inside. And the architecture was beautiful. In heaven it seems that the architecture of the day has pillars—large pillars. Every home had large porches with pillars in front of it and huge archways. Some of the homes were made out of what seemed to be a brick or stone type of material. Some were made out of a wood-type material. Yet, as I looked, there were no nails or even pegs. Not a piece was sawn but everything was crafted somehow and fit perfectly together. The fit was so perfect, no nails were needed. It was as if the house had formed itself into existence.

I saw a veranda in one home that looked like onyx stone. You could see through it. It was clear as glass. Inlaid in the porch were precious stones and gold and silver (the things we hold so dear) and there were great diamonds. Everything is so beautiful, but they all dim at the very look of Jesus. When you see Him, even the beautiful architecture of heaven dims to look on His wonderful face. Just one glimpse of Him and everything dims in comparison. He is the expressed image of the Father and all of heaven revolves around the Lord and His great mercy.

Colossians 1:15
He is the image of the invisible God; his is the primacy over all creation.
[REB]

I saw several large cities in heaven and in each city were large streets. One particular area I was going to I knew had seven main streets that ran towards the Throne. They were huge streets. But the architecture was indescribable.

I saw a home made of clear stone with roses that were alive and growing and yet were imbedded in the stones. And they gave off the most beautiful aroma.

43

You could put your ear up to anything solid in heaven and you could hear it humming the most beautiful songs. Some of the songs we have here; some we don't. Everything gives praise and glory to the Lord.

There was another home I was taken to that was just off the main street where I was walking. I was weeping with joy. I was joining in the joy and happiness of everybody. This home was not as big as some of the others, but it was a fine home. If it were possible to build on earth it would cost at least 45 trillion dollars—if it were possible to build. It was bigger than the White House. The angels told me I had to stop here. "Somebody wants to talk to you."

I walked up to the door and it was my grandfather's house. He was sitting on the front porch and Grandma was there too. I remember falling down on my knees and saying, "Grandpa." He stood up and it was as though he was 28 or 30 years old. When he died, he was 97. Now, he was in perfect health and so was Grandma. We hugged and I just didn't know what to say. After a few moments, they said, "Richard, you have an appointment with God, but you will be back. Your home is just over yonder." And

A Place Called Heaven

they pointed down the street and there was
an open place for a home to be built. I have
never thought I have done anything to
deserve all the goodness God has shown
me, especially this. Suddenly, I was gone
from them. I knew they were smiling. They
knew what was going on. They had been
told.

I saw many homes on that street for people
that I loved and who loved me. I saw some
of the great Generals in God's Army. I saw
Jack Coe. He wasn't sick and he wasn't as
heavy as in life. And he was teaching. He
was standing in a crowd of people with a
loud booming voice. He just waved at me
and I waved back. There wasn't time to
talk.

I also saw William Branham. He was sitting
by himself talking with the Lord. I didn't
want to interrupt him. He just gave me a
wave and I waved back. And Jesus looked
at me and smiled and I knew what He was
saying, "He will be back. He is just visiting."

I saw other people that had died and had
gone to be with Jesus. Other great
preachers down through the ages; I saw
them. They were out among the people,
encouraging them, telling of the great

wonders of heaven and the great things God had done for them. Some of them had been there a long time, but they were still learning. Just like little children, they were soaking up something they wanted to learn so bad. Then the angel on the left said, "We have to go toward the Throne," and we were gone.

Everything in heaven flows into the Throne. However you get there, all traffic flows to the Throne: from the veil; in the beautiful conveyances; coming down from the sky. However God brings you into heaven, all of heaven runs to the Throne.

People in heaven clamor to get to the Throne and to talk to Jesus. They may be standing on the street corner looking down the street and Jesus might be walking down it. In wonderment they exclaim, "He is coming. He is coming our way. We are going to get to talk to Him."

I saw Jesus many times talking with people and He would turn and look at me. I wanted to talk to Him but I knew that I had to wait my turn. I felt great peace. Always when I saw Him, I had a desire to get before God on the Throne.

SIX
Archives of heaven

One very large building had a huge archway. I was taken into it. Inside were rows upon rows of shelves with books. The books were 15 feet tall. This was a library. This was the Archives of Heaven where the other books are kept.

The shelves were miles long and miles high. And there were hundreds of angels servicing the books. They were going in and out—lots of activity. These are the different books about our lives and these are the books that are taken to God when judgment time comes. These books are the records of our works here on earth. If a person sins, it is recorded in the book.

I was given the understanding that when we repent, anything that was done wrong or sinful in nature that is recorded in the books is erased from the books for eternity. No one can find the record, not even God.

I saw another very large building, different from the archives. In that building is a book corresponding to every person on earth. There are other books about our lives including even our thoughts. It is a pictorial record of our lives: every thought, every reaction, everything is recorded in heaven. These are the "other books" mentioned in Revelation. God keeps records.

Revelation 20:12
And I saw the dead, great and small, standing before the throne, and books were opened. Another book was opened, which is the book of life. The dead were judged according to what they had done as recorded in the books. [NIV]

There are many books for each person—many different books. Tall, slender angels take care of the huge books. They are 8-9 feet tall. And they write in the books using a golden quill that is five feet long and could write forever. An angel would hold the book in his right hand and make the record with his left.

An angel would pull out a book with his left hand and open the thick pages. In each page is something like a video screen except the images are three-dimensional. The images contain the history of life. And the books were written—the picture was created—before time.

Psalm 139:16

Your eyes foresaw my deeds, and they were all recorded in your book; my life was fashioned before it had come into being.
[REB]

God can go forward or backward in time. He created time; He invented it. God sets up our tomorrows because of our prayers and seeking God today. God knows our tomorrows. He orders our tomorrows. But He orders them because we pray today. He knows what is coming tomorrow. If we pray today, God gives us our tomorrows by a system of weights and measures. We can know what is coming tomorrow because of the checks and balances within us. He causes us to pray and to seek God. Invariably, when we are praying about tomorrow or what is going to happen down the line, it is because God has a blessing in store for us and the devil wants to steal it away or trip us up. When we get in prayer, it loosens God to go into our tomorrows and lay a trap for the devil and make sure our blessings are right there, right on time. This is something I was told by the Lord when I was in heaven.

I was also told that all of our tomorrows are God's yesterdays.

I was taken to a place that I don't understand. I was standing on the edge of the universe and I saw all the universe as a great spiral. From this vantage point it looked like a huge clock spring wound up. The center was pure white and the light got dimmer and dimmer as it got out where I was: on the edge. I was closer to this than others. I could see people way behind me and they thought they were close. People up ahead also thought they were close, but they were ahead of people in time. Then I learned a lesson about seeking God. Men everywhere ought to seek God and be thankful for where they are with God. Do not be envious of others who may be a little bit ahead. Pray for those who are a little bit behind you. But all together, we form a group that is seeking God.

Hebrews 10:25
Let us not give up meeting together, as some are in the habit of doing, but let us encourage one another-and all the more as

you see the Day approaching. [NIV]

The Word tells us not to forsake the assembling of yourselves together, more so as we see that day is fast approaching. There is strength in numbers and when you are seeking God, the greater the anointing and the easier it is to pray. I learned this. And God is way ahead of us because our tomorrows are God's yesterdays. He has already laid victory in our path. Holy Spirit makes us aware (if you are really close to God) that you need to pray because there is something in your pathway you need to be aware of. How many times has He done this for all of us? I don't know. I can tell you about myself. Many times He has and I have always been better off about praying about tomorrow knowing God is there already. He is going to take care of me if I take special pains to pray TODAY.

There are things in heaven that I saw for myself, that I was told by the angels with me, that God created before the beginning of time. Before He invented time, He finished heaven, the host of heaven, and He created the blessings I would need when I got there.

One of the stores I was in had clothing that was exactly what I would need in heaven. I had my own section. God created everything that I would have need of in heaven before time was even invented. He knew I would be there.

Yet, there were other places in heaven where I saw homes being built. Angels at work, people busy at work, creating homes and putting blessings there that we couldn't receive on earth—the blessings are received in heaven.

SEVEN
Library of God's Knowledge

Another building I was taken to contained the written part of God's knowledge. He wrote some of his knowledge so that we would have something to relate to. There were individual symbols with each having the interpretation of the symbol written by God. When here, your mind is automatically stimulated.

I talked with one man who was there. "Brother Richard, I have been here for two millennia and I've only gotten to page two."

Millions of angels come and go to the library. And as many people who are inhabitants of heaven. The angels were coming back to earth. Many times in this life we don't know what to do and we pray for wisdom. The Bible says that angels are ministers to the heirs of salvation. They go to the Library of God's Knowledge and get

53

wisdom. This is where they go to get it. And we can receive it. Sometimes it is brought strictly by the Holy Spirit Himself.

Hebrews 1:14
Are not all angels ministering spirits sent to serve those who will inherit salvation? [NIV]

People in heaven have access to it and never forget.

There were great universities in heaven—I mean GREAT—and there are many of them. Our education is not complete when we leave earth. We have only just begun.

I saw two giant buildings. These were colleges for people. They are taught by angels and people. All subjects were taught. Even singing. Every song, every note, every word you are taught stays with you throughout eternity. There is no end to learning. All of your mind is illuminated to the wisdom and knowledge of heaven. 100% of your mind is used—and it is increasing in capability. You can do anything in heaven that your heart desires to do because your desire is for the things that are right.

The university buildings were a mile or two long and a mile or two deep. They are great buildings that would contain hundreds and hundreds of thousands of people. The classrooms were huge auditoriums. I could see them through the windows as I walked by. I could hear the people learning and praising God inside. And I was told that anything you learn, you never forget.

I remember standing for just a moment in utter amazement. I could hear everything that was said. People were praising God and the secrets of God were being made known. When you are in heaven, there are no secrets about God.

Sigmund

EIGHT
Memorials

In my tour, I was taken to a building like a huge, layered wedding cake. The bottom layer was big and round and about 15 feet tall. It had a lit archway. Above the archway there was a name. I went in.

Inside were walls that were running revival scenes over and over. These were the revivals I had been involved with since I was a child. They were being played over and over and God was continually getting the glory.

In 3-inch letters it was written:

"THE GLORY GOD GETS OUT OF RICHARD'S LIFE."

I saw other memorials. In Cornelius' memorial, there was much almsgiving. I saw his memorial. It looked a lot like the Washington Monument, but not as tall. It had written language on it and angels were standing there making announcements about the almsgiving that Cornelius did. It was a place where people came to see what was mentioned in the Bible. I never saw Cornelius. I don't know what he looked like. But I felt in my spirit that he wasn't very far away from me. He was just talking with people and giving God the glory.

There were more memorials everywhere. Each memorial would depict some great victory that one of God's children would win down here on earth. Memorials told when someone—a real bad sinner—came to Christ. Memorials told when some great battle was fought and won for the glory of God's Spirit. I saw a memorial about a service that Billy Graham held in southern California. It told about the glory that God received there and the number of people that were saved and the words were sealed in God forever.

I saw other memorials—it was a glorious place to be. I saw Smith Wigglesworth's. I did not get to talk with him. He was at a distance, but he looked my way and smiled waving his hand. He was busy with people. He was directing them here and there and telling them how much God loved them and what He had in store for them in heaven.

Smith was doing in heaven what he did on earth: helping people. Since there are no sick people in heaven for him to pray for, he was talking with all the new arrivals who had read his books and heard him speak and wanted to talk to him. But he was very humble going about his business of helping others.

Matthew 23:11

The greatest among you
will be your servant. [NIV]

He that would be the greatest among you, let him be the servant of all. That is one of the rules that heaven is run by. You are a servant of all; you are a servant to all; and a servant of the Lord. The way to get up with God is to get down and get beyond yourself to where there is nothing of you left. The death of self is much in the sight of God.

I was told by the angels that were with me, that there are things that God highly prizes. He highly prizes someone who is absolutely truthful, totally honest, and prays before he makes any decision and makes sure that all of his decisions are what God wants him to make. God highly prizes someone who will pray and seek Him

59

in all things and be obedient. Above all is obedience to God. Those things are principals that heaven is run by.

NINE
Johann Sebastian Bach

God does not want to lose one bit of talent and skill developed on earth. And when that talent is brought to heaven, it is multiplied a million-fold.

I saw and heard Johann Sebastian Bach on a huge organ that had notes below and above what people normally hear; and I heard all of it. And as he played, the choirs of heaven joined in praise and worship—everyone joined in the music.

I noticed something else: music everywhere. The people in the various villages and cities were praising God and it was in song. One village would have one song. Another village yet another song. But as I went up in the air, I could hear music from the different villages at the same time and they were all singing in perfect harmony with each other. The higher I went, the more villages I could hear and everyone was singing the same song in harmony with

61

each other.

I saw choirs from a distance. Then I saw them closer. I had heard them in the background and I had seen smaller groups singing. Sometimes the choirs were groups of angels singing. Apparently, one of the songs was specifically for me. While I was there, I knew what it was. Now, I do not understand the song, the meaning, nor do I remember any of it nor what was said. It was only for me to know while I was there.

I saw that the songs angels sang had something to do with ministry and something to do with what God was saying to those people in heaven.

The songs that the people were singing were different. Sometimes groups were two or three. Sometimes they were large groups. I saw a large group in an amphitheater setting and they seemed to be standing on air even though it also looked like risers. They were singing songs like what we have here.

One song I remember is "The King is Coming." But their words were different: "The King Has Come." They went through the whole story from heaven's point of view and it was a most beautiful song. I remember hearing it, but I don't remember all the words.

When you leave heaven, you lose the ability to understand things that they say there. Much of it you don't remember because you don't have the words to speak it. You are no longer speaking in that heavenly language anytime you want. And people totally understand you.

I heard a Russian sounding language spoken by groups of people and other people who I knew were not Russian could walk up to them and speak perfectly in that dialect. Yet, they spoke in a heavenly dialect—and they spoke in English perfectly. It seems you have the ability of all languages plus heaven's own language.

The closer I got to the Throne of God, the greater the number of people in the choirs. I remember a choir of 50-60 thousand. [While I was there, I knew the exact number, but now I don't know.] They sang with the deepest bass and the highest soprano—beyond the ranges of anyone on earth. They could be heard all over heaven pleasantly in the background. It was music in the language of God.

There is an oasis in heaven. It is a city on a peninsula that goes out into the ocean.

The City of God has what looks like beautiful apartment buildings. I saw a waterfall coming off of one building.

There are stores in heaven, but they are unique stores. They are aimed specifically at the person walking through the door. There was a jewelry store. The diamonds represented a woman in a man's life. One store I walked into had only suits and gowns specifically tailored to me. Very specific to my desires.

In one store I saw garments that had been made before the beginning of time. These were made and put on the shelf and were in pristine perfect condition as if they had just been put there. Of course, no one would disturb them because they were for someone else. It is for your joy to make sure that they get what God has for them. I believe that the clothing being made were rewards that are being heaped up in heaven. In heaven, God rewards back those things that we give here that are only known by God. He knows what we give in secret. I saw this.

Matthew 6:3-4
But when you give to the needy, do not let your left hand know what your right hand is doing, so that your giving may be in secret. Then your Father, who sees what is done in secret, will reward you. [NIV]

I saw what was some kind of center or gathering place in heaven; like a community center. There were thousands of people—women—sitting at tables and benches in a park-like setting. In the center of them was a pile of beautiful clothing. They were sewing. But they did not have a needle in their hand. They were just putting pieces of cloth together and telling them what to be. And it would be what they said. They were making garments for people who were soon to be there.

Dress in heaven varied. Some were dressed in some sort of a pants and pull over shirt: purely white. One outfit I saw was bright yellow. I saw others of different colors. I saw people dressed in suits similar to what we wear here on earth but much more expensive. Clothing was made out of heavenly material. Yet, I saw people dressed like one would think an angel would dress: long flowing robes.

I saw the Lord many times. He had gold around the ends of His sleeves and around His collar. He also had a golden waist band and gold around the hem of his long flowing robe. It is the style of the clothes in heaven.

I cannot put into words how beautiful it was to see all these different people with the fabulous adornments. It was because of the anointing; no where did I see jewelry hanging off of people. It wasn't necessary. The glow of God's presence just makes a person beautiful.

"I want to see God," I heard myself say. The angel corrected me. "No. You have an appointment." Angels do not go before God unless they are bidden.

TEN
Chimes in heaven

I was shown chimes in heaven.

They were very, very loud and beautiful. They were like a huge minaret and tree-like and they were everywhere. The pipes of the chimes were huge with deep full sound that filled the air with the harmonies of a chime and you could hear them at a great distance. And they were playing. I was told that whenever someone got saved, they made a sound.

At one time I was many hundred or maybe even thousands of feet in the air being shown around heaven. Being high up and looking down, I could see many chimes. They were multicolored. Some of the chimes had glory coming out of them. They were like the crystal Diadem tree and gave off a wavering sound that was beautiful. It was like an organ playing continually. They would always chime with a loud and beautiful song—yes—every time somebody

67

got saved.

I saw the chimes near the balconies of heaven. There were seven large chimes there. Seven large towers with chimes hanging off of them. The saints of God would go to the balconies and begin to pray and worship God. Looking down they could see their promises coming to pass. Or they would look in on a revival meeting as they often did, they would say "Preach it preacher." They were joining in with the service. The chimes behind them would start to give off the most beautiful heavenly sound: a song of worship and praise.

Now, here on earth there have been times in revival services where we have heard the anthems of glory being sung in heaven and the beautiful music in heaven being played along. From my point of view, from what I saw, we heard the chimes that were near the balconies of heaven playing those beautiful songs. We could hear them. In those services, our praise and worship reached high enough to co-mingle with those that were coming down from heaven. Then there was a steady flow of God's Spirit. Oh, to be set in high places with Christ Jesus. This is what this scripture means. We can be set in those heavenly places if we pay the price to stay in the Spirit of God.

Ephesians 2:6

And hath raised us up together,
and made us sit together in heavenly places
in Christ Jesus: [KJV]

Sigmund

ELEVEN
Family groups waiting

I walked by groups and groups of people and I could hear them talking. It was like the buzzing and busyness of people waiting at an airport or a train station. They were obviously waiting for someone. And they were preparing something also.

"We did this because we knew he would like it."

"Wait until he sees this."

It became obvious these people were involved in the preparation of a mansion. And it was a mansion for a member of their family. These groups were talking about a family member—a friend—who was about to arrive. And they had helped prepare his mansion for him.

Oh, the excitement they had in anticipation of someone coming home. There were announcement centers that looked like band shells except they were made out of glory clouds. It was solid yet you could see through it and it seemed as though it lit up from the inside with a great amount of the glory that permeated everywhere. Solid and full of glory and the glory would pass through: all different colors; like fire shooting through it; amber and gold; sparkles and aroma. The fragrance of God.

At this band shell, someone was announcing that someone was coming home. There were a great number of people in the crowd and I knew it was a pastor coming home after a lot of years of service to his church. He was on the way to the band shell. He had already come through the veil. And there was such joy and wonderment in the people.

There are balconies and bleachers in heaven that look over the events on earth. People come to watch prayers come to pass. They are the "cloud of witnesses."

Hebrews 12:1
*Therefore, since we are surrounded by
such a great cloud of witnesses,
let us throw off everything that hinders
and the sin that so easily entangles,
and let us run with perseverance the race*

marked out for us. [NIV]

They watch births and weddings. They are a cheering section hollering out encouragement to us. Right desires have positive creative force.

I was always accompanied by at least two angels; one on the right and another on the left. The one on the right mostly explained things. The one on the left didn't say much except the continual reminder that I had an appointment with God. Separate jobs, but in perfect harmony.

The angel on the right told me about a rewards department in heaven. I did not see it and did not go there. But it was explained to me and I heard others talking about it.

It is a huge records building. This is where records are kept of the rewards that we do not receive on earth for some reason or other. An example would be the reward for giving to others or almsgiving to the Lord. Because of the love and compassion we have in our hearts, we give to the greater need. What we give here will be received back in heaven. There is a rewards department in heaven.

I was taken to a large building, large even by heaven's standards. There were many rooms inside and the rooms were beautifully decorated. The furniture was extraordinary—beyond description. I saw what looked to be a chair similar to a recliner. I didn't get to sit in it but I saw someone sit. As he did, the chair molded itself around him providing tremendous comfort.

A book was given to him and he began to read it out loud to others around him. I don't know what he was reading—I wasn't allowed to hear it—but everyone was smiling and praising God. I really felt that within this book contained the desires and the wants and wishes of some Christians here on earth. Plans were being laid according to what was written in the book. The way he was a blessing to others, he was going to be blessed in heaven. And they were planning his home where he was going to live. They were planning the heavenly events for him. God had made it known and had it written in this book.

I believe that what you made happen to others while on earth will happen to you in heaven. In this one building—in this one room—were the intentions of God for the works of one man and how God was going to bless him. The building was about the desire of God to bless even more than we can desire to receive from Him.

There were other rooms in this huge building. And the rooms were mammoth, sometimes beyond description in size. Some of the rooms had huge chandeliers in the middle from the ceiling. There were three chandeliers in the first room that we were in where the man was sitting in the chair. Each one was several hundred feet across and they were lit with a glow from within. There was no electricity but they glowed beautifully. Like the Diadem tree, they continually glowed in different colors with what was almost like bursts of fire. They glowed and gave off energy. The energy seemed to go through everything in heaven. I believe it was the Shekinah glory of God. The Lamb is the light: the power and presence of God.

All three chandeliers were doing the same thing at the same time. Across this huge, huge room, and all through the room there were people reading to other people out of books, and they were planning, and I heard one of them say, "Now let's do this." And he made a gesture in the air, and when he made a gesture in the air, arcs of what looked like fire, sprang off of his hand and it sparked like fireworks that hung in the air for a few moments. I thought, "Wow, I wish I could do that."

One of the angels that stood by me heard my thoughts and said that in heaven you have the ability to do things that you can't even think of on earth. You can do it in heaven because it pleases God. In heaven the laws that govern earth are done away with and the laws of heaven govern everything. And that's all he said about it.

But I had realized then that anything that is possible in heaven that gives glory, honor and praise to the Lord can be a reward for things done on earth; especially in this room. In heaven, you receive rewards for things done without reward on earth. I am also told that those who don't seek rewards on earth receive the biggest rewards in heaven. That is what these people were doing. They were planning the rewards out of these books that are written, spoken, and recorded by the Lord.

There were many other rooms, but I was not allowed to go into them. The gentle reminder was always there, "You have an appointment with God." I had to stick to the path. The angel would say "No, you must be about the Father's business."

I really wanted to see this other large building because somehow I knew that it contained all the miracles that we need on earth for our bodies. I don't know the law, but I do know that God created everything we have need of for our bodies. In this building and other large buildings there appeared to be factories. I don't know or can't describe what was done there. No stacks. No power lines. Just worship and praise coming from them. I could hear it. And there were lots of people coming and going in and out of the buildings.

For a "factory," the architecture was beautiful: spires, arched doorways, columns all around. This was the typical architecture of heaven. But off in the distance I could see the Temple of God, the biggest building in heaven and the most beautiful. Every time I would look in that direction, something would stir within me. "I have an appointment with God."

Sigmund

TWELVE
Jesus came my way

Where did the water come from?" I wondered. There were fountains everywhere, but there was no plumbing. There are no bathrooms. None of the houses I saw had bathrooms. You don't have to eat. And if you did eat, you don't have to go to the bathroom anyway. You don't even need to take a bath. You just don't have to in heaven.

Some of the fountains were the size of a city block. Some of them were almost a crystal—you could see right through them. They looked like ice, but were not. They were some kind of crystal. The figures in them were alive—they moved.

At another fountain, there were hundreds of people standing around watching. The water turned hundreds of different colors and flowed down over this beautiful mountain with trees. The water squirted up into the air and came down in a mist over it.

The mist clung to the trees like tinsel does on a Christmas tree. It sparkled. Yet, the trees on the mountain were the most vivid green and other colors. The water wasn't like water we have here—and yet it was. It was water, but it could do anything you wanted it to do. It turned into ice that was not cold. There were sheets of ice on the trees that were dazzling. I could not tell where the water drained. There were no pipes in the ground.

There is no electric current, but there are lights everywhere. Big chandeliers. No shadows. Nothing in heaven casts a shadow. The light is even from every direction. The Lamb is the light, thereof. There is no shadow, no variableness, no shadow of failing in heaven. We have shadows here because things can fail here. Things cannot fail in heaven. They are set for eternity.

James 1:17
Every good gift and every perfect gift is from above, and cometh down from the Father of lights, with whom is no variableness, neither shadow of turning.
[KJV]

There are thousands of fountains in heaven and they depict different things. One I saw had a statue of Jesus holding a pitcher. He was pouring out the great big pitcher and glory was coming out. The glory was falling on little children and grown ups—they had their hand up wanting a drink. The statues were somehow alive for they moved, yet they were made out of stone. I could see Jesus in the distance and the image of Him moving in a fountain right in front of me. How does stone live? And Jesus looked at me and smiled.

The closer I got to the Throne, the greater the wonders were.

I saw Jesus coming my way. I stopped and the angels stood at attention and backed away from me a couple feet. Then they bowed low, backed up and stood at attention with looks of adoration on their faces. Jesus walked in my direction and I fell on my face like a deadman. He stopped a few feet from me and I remember looking at the nail holes through His ankles and His feet. They shone with a light from the inside of beautiful, beautiful Jesus. He suffered this for me. I had no words.

Evidently he touched me and I was able to

stand. I did not feel worthy to stand or to look at His face. He reached out His fingers and lifted my chin and said, "Son. Look at Me. I love you. Even though you have been disobedient and haven't done what I have told you to do, I still love you and I desire for you to tell my people about this place called heaven. I desire for you to tell my people the glorious things that my Father has made for them that they might want to come here. I have chosen you and ordained you for this one work above all others that I might speak to you on this day of these things."

He took my hand and began to walk with me like a father would a little child. We walked a little further down the street and He said, "I have many things to tell you. I will come to you again in just a short time. I have something else to tell you, but right now, there is more for you to see. More for you to witness and experience. Tell my people I am coming soon. I love them." Then He gave me a big hug and kissed me on the cheek and said, "I love you, too."

He held His hands out in front of me and I saw His palms, the nail scars in His wrists and His hands. The wounds were open, shining with a beautiful light. I saw my name written in His hand, carved almost like a knife had carved it.

"See," He said, "Your name is carved in my hand." I knew then what that scripture meant.

Isaiah 49:16
See, I have engraved you on the palms of my hands; your walls are ever before me.
[NIV]

Then He looked at me again and said, "I have more to tell you later." Again He said this. And He said, "Go with the angels. They are going to take you to see more people and see more things. I have an appointment and I have to go. My Father wants me. I must go. I am always obedient to my Father." Suddenly He was gone. He just vanished out of sight and was gone. In a fraction of a moment I saw Him off in the distance walking and talking with people going toward the Throne.

Then the angels came back around me.

Sigmund

THIRTEEN
City of God

I had been walking all this time. Now something really different happened—I went up. I was going up through what looked like clouds, but they were groups of people. I could see the entire city. The higher I got, the more of heaven I could see and it was a busy, busy place. In the distance, I could see the Throne of God.

Around, there were mountains that had to be 50,000 feet tall. And they had snow. The snow never melted even though the temperature was always just right. I was taken to the base of the mountain.

The mountains were covered with terraced parks. And I noticed what I was told were "conveyances." These conveyances floated like a boat in the sky. They were carved wood and metallic. And people sat in them and talked with each other as they floated around.

I was taken to the ocean; the Sea of God's Glory. It was crystal clear and in places seemed to have no bottom. There were millions of people in the water and under the water. They couldn't drown and people were playing under the water. One guy had built a castle out of rocks on the bottom of the ocean.

And there were more conveyances that were like boats in the water. It was as if these "vehicles" were pastime building projects of someone who wanted to make conveyances.

From up in the air I could see the City of God and the villages surrounding the city out into the country side. There were villages of many different styles just as there are around the world today. But all were clean and beautiful with flowing fountains everywhere. I saw buildings suspended in the air thousands of feet above the ground.

It is as though heaven is layered. There was a layer, an atmosphere and thousands of feet of air and then there was another layer with an atmosphere and thousands of feet of air. I don't know how big it was. I was taken up 30-40 thousand feet and yet it was just a skip in the air.

In heaven, you can be anywhere in moments of time. You could take a leisurely stroll to the layers just walking through the air.

Wherever I went, angels and people were around. Sometimes just a few. Sometimes large groups. All were standing around talking with great joy and worshiping. At times they were laughing with hilarious joy evidently over a loved one coming home or a promise that had come to pass. And they were always talking about Jesus. I can still see Him going here and there among the people.

There was an auditorium that was an announcement center. The Lord Himself was on stage. He was with me and I could look down and see Him as He was with groups of people walking through the air. He was in heaven and in heaven there is only Jesus and He is omnipresent. And instantly at the right moment, He was on the stage of the auditorium. It might have seated 10 million people. I looked and He was there, always, and right now.

The stage was beautiful. There was a throne-chair on it and I believe that was where Jesus was sitting before He suddenly stood. There was no pulpit, but there was an area that was both gold and silver and had precious jewels. There was a fragrance—an aroma that was indescribable and beyond measure—the fragrance of God Himself.

The auditorium was open to the sky and there was a stage. There were bleachers and seats, beautiful seats that were hand-carved and unbelievably comfortable to sit in. Anything you sit on in heaven is comfortable forever.

The Lord suddenly was there on the stage of gold, ivory and silver and material I don't know. I was given the understanding that there are other theaters throughout heaven where announcements are made. But this was the theater where Jesus announced that He was going to be born of a virgin.

Someplace in heaven, there is a re-enactment of the manger and virgin birth to the Glory of God—an eternal Nativity that declares the miracle: God became man.

Someplace in heaven you can feel and hear the throbbing heart of God, loving, yearning, churning—you can feel His deep loving compassion. We think of the Word as the most God will do for us, but it is not. He limited Himself. We cannot comprehend the capacity of God—in heaven there are no limits. He will do everything in His Word. The sacrifice of His Son indicates that He was and is willing to do everything to redeem us.

In heaven there is no yesterday, no tomorrow, just right now. The "right now" situation needed Jesus there in the auditorium and that is where He was. He walked on stage to thunderous praise and worship and adoration that seemed to go on forever. It was glorious.

Jesus stood there and looked so lovingly at the people. He just looked at them and loved them. You could feel the Shekinah glory love that came out of him. It was awesome. Words fail.

Slowly, the people quieted down and there came a quietness: a holy hush over the auditorium. He was about to speak. Suddenly a deep bass voice—the sound I have heard so often—like rushing waters, metallic, deep bass voice—began to speak. I do not know what He said now; I was not allowed to remember it. But I do know the topic was Eternity and what it means to

God and what God has in store for His people. It was awesome.

FOURTEEN
Mysteries of God

I had lots of questions. There were things I just wanted to know.

While floating up in the sky, I saw other levels of heaven. I didn't understand. When we started floating up into the sky another level of heaven appeared with ground, buildings and sky. But I couldn't see it from the first level.

I knew that there were other continents, islands and oceans far away. I was not allowed to know anything about them, but I knew they existed. Some have asked if there is life on other planets. Yes. And there are vast places in heaven where people will never go. And there are governments in heaven even though it is an absolute Theocracy.

There were streets that I wanted to go down—I wanted to look at other things—but I was not allowed. I could only talk to a few people. There were buildings that I couldn't go into. Some, I was told, people would never be allowed into.

I marveled at the children. They were so advanced and yet still children. Apparently, people even in heaven have to grow. And they grew at different rates.

I wondered where the lumber came from for the buildings because no tree has ever been cut in heaven. Who made the bricks? What was made in the factories? They were huge.

I learned the Diadem trees were made before the creation of the earth. I thought to myself that I could find out how old the earth is by asking how old the Diadem trees were. That was to remain a mystery—I was not allowed to know. But they were miles in diameter. Had they been growing since the beginning of creation? Or were they made that way?

It was a mystery to me how the animals communicated. There were birds singing "Amazing Grace." And I knew every language along with a heavenly language and could speak to anyone with perfect understanding. How could this be?

There were people there who had not died yet. I have heard others say that about heaven. I saw them. And I wondered about this mystery.

Continents, oceans, transparent buildings full of people, kitchens without cooking, factories without power lines, angels with supernatural strength. My list went on and on and kept growing. I wanted to know but was not allowed to know. I knew there was something, but what it was, I didn't know. I asked and asked the angels who were guiding me. Regularly they told me, "It is not for you to know at this time."

Finally, after many, many questions—mysteries I wanted to know about—the angel on my right who was doing most of the talking looked at me and sternly said, "The mysteries of God are none of your business."

Sigmund

FIFTEEN
Prophetic heaven

Heaven is a big place. There are areas in heaven that are prophetic.

I saw the black tornado of judgment. I saw revival and judgment.

There was an area that had the landscape of Colorado with mountains, trees, rocks and rivers. And there was a white-pine pulpit. Two fists came through the sky between the Shekinah glory. The right hand was gold and was God's blessing. The left hand was steel: God's judgment.

I saw the Falls of God's Glory. One stream of water falling into vapor on earth. We on earth can rise up to that level. We can rise into the mist of the Falls of God's Glory.

And I saw the Tidal Wave: the last great move of God. It was seven tiers tall. Prophetically, I was told seven signs:
1—the last great move of God will be in out-

of-the-way places, day and night.

2—signs and wonders will increase and be fought against.

3—laws of physics will be suspended so the miraculous can flow.

4—laws of time and space will be made known to men.

5—knowledge of man shall increase and never be based on fleshly things.

6—seven-fold tidal wave: the last great move of God breaking on the shores of eternity; the greatest part will be poured out in rural areas; "I seek my bride in humble places. I was born in a stable."

7—awareness is given my people in days and weeks just before my return.

Mass multitudes will be involved. The revival will be through people who give all praise to the Lord. It is coming to root out and destroy the phony. It will keep the faithful and it will be the introduction to the Coming of Christ

I saw Abraham's amphitheater. It was like a football arena only hundreds of times larger. In it was a cloud in the "playing field." In the cloud I could see all the promises that have come to pass for and because of Abraham. The promises were to us and the entire world, not just the Jews.

There were 2-3 million seats with names on them. People had specific promises. Promises related to David's throne and the lineage of kings.

Each of the patriarchs had an amphitheater. The angels helped people remember the promises.

On the way to the Throne there was the Amphitheater of David. I didn't go into his building, but I knew about it when I went by. Somehow I sensed in my spirit, I knew—as in heaven you just know things—that was where David and his descendants went to see their promises coming to pass. But, everyone is welcome.

I saw a building in the shape of a castle like a cornucopia (horn of plenty). It was a Prayer Center. Angels were traveling in and out of the archway at the "speed of light." Going through the archway was going into the presence of God. The angels were carrying golden censers that carried prayers. They held them by the bowl of the censer. The prayers are precious cargo and are treated as such.

No prayer goes unanswered—even wrong prayer. The prayers are brought before the face of God.

Instantly, the angels go back for more.

SIXTEEN
Classes of angels

I saw at least 70 classes of angels.

I first became aware of just how many there were when I was walking on the golden pathway and smelled the fragrance that renewed my strength. I noticed more and more angels of every description and I believe every rank. They were busy with the people and were everywhere and were beautiful. Some were in groups; others were by themselves. All were busy doing the business of heaven. As they did their business, they would stop every few feet and bow their heads giving silent praise and worship to God.

But I noticed something: there is no such thing as tomorrow and no such thing as yesterday. It was and is always right now.

I asked one of the angels how time is measured in heaven. He looked at me with a puzzled look on his face. He said, "You mean time as you know it?"

"Yes."

He continued, "Time here is not measured in such trivial things as years, but in ages where the glory of God rolls forever."

That settled that subject in a big hurry.

The angels took on a new meaning to me.

The classes of angels look like they are family members.

Some wore shirts with draw strings. Some wore pants. Some had shoes. Their hair was never longer than their ear. None had shaved heads, but some had beards. They looked like they were 28-30 human-years old.

I saw some angels that were 12-15 feet tall and as wide as 4 or 5 of the biggest line-backers on any NFL team. Some had swords. Some did not. But the angels I saw were huge. I was told that they were warfaring angels on their way to do battle. I stopped, bowed my head, and backed up a bit. But the angels with me and the voice behind me with a gentle touch said, "You have nothing to fear. They are about the

Father's business."

Then I noticed groups of angels. Some were tall and slender. One of them I had seen before in several visions I have had in my life. He was there. It was the first time I had noticed him. He was standing off to the side watching everything that I did and everything that I said. And he had a large book. He was writing in it with a quill that must have been six feet long—it was huge. And golden. The book he was writing in was made out of some type of golden-looking material and must have weighed several hundred pounds. But he held it in his left hand, writing with his right. It was like it weighed nothing to him.

I know I had seen him before. Now the word tells me that every thought and every deed and every action that we do on earth, God keeps a record of. I wondered at this when I saw this angel writing. Now I understand that everyone has an angel or angels that record everything that they say or do—and God knows it. In Revelation we find that the "books are opened."

Revelation 20:12
And I saw the dead, great and small, standing before the throne, and books were

*opened. Another book was opened, which is
the book of life. The dead were judged
according to what they had done as
recorded in the books.* [NIV]

I saw what I call the Armies of God. I was
taken to a very large area that wasn't in the
city. I don't know where it was and I don't
know what part of heaven it was in, but I
was taken there in an instant. I was in the
air and looked down on possibly hundreds
of thousands of angels lined up in ranks
and in units. They looked just like soldiers
getting ready to go on parade.

I knew—I understood—that they were
standing where they were standing when
God created them for the purpose He
created them. They were God's warfaring
angels and they would leave and come down
and fight battles for us. Then they would go
back and stand in formation until they were
needed again. Some of them had swords
that were 15 feet long and on fire. The
swords looked like they were of flaming
material. These angels were not what you
would call tall and slender like I saw in
parts of heaven. Nor were they friendly
looking and kindly looking like some of
them I saw in heaven and still see today.

I have seen these before. God has shown them to me while I am here but not so much as the other types of angels. These were fearsome angels dressed in battle garb. They didn't have helmets, but they had huge shields, flaming swords, and they had spears that were 30 feet long. These are big, big angels. They must have stood 20 feet tall and in our weight probably the better part of a ton. They were huge muscular angels. They looked like a Mr. America but considerably larger.

Some of them had short-sleeved garments on. Some of them had long-sleeved garments. Others were dressed in something like a tunic and pants type of outfit with draw strings around the neck. Others were clothed with just light.

They had supernatural weapons that I do not know how to explain. I knew that some of them could speak words and cause whole nations to just crumble and fall into the sea. They were armed, some with words, some with swords, some with spears that had special purposes, and all with the power of God. And they knew their jobs—their highly specialized jobs. Nobody had to tell them how to do it. God just told them where to do it.

103

Some of them were clothed with the power to move the earth. Others were clothed with the power to bring judgment, but they all had power to defend and to keep God's children.

I looked down and I said, "Look at those mighty angels."

The angels standing with me stood at attention and said, "Behold the warfaring angels of God. They are mighty to the pulling down of the strongholds of the evil one."

I noticed all their hands were clothed with power and I asked, "Why are their hands aflame?" I was told that they were ready at any moment to come and do battle against the powers of the devil that assail against us. They are ready at any moment to come and be on assignment to deliver from the power of the devil. The power of God is in their hands to accomplish all that God wants them to do.

They were mighty and they were lined up rank and file: hundreds and hundreds and hundreds of them. I looked at them and knew that they were released to fight for us the minute we mention the name of Jesus.

I saw thousands of them coming and going from their rank and file and their place where they stood to come and do battle on earth. They would come out of the ranks almost at the speed of light and disappear. I knew that they were coming to earth to help someone.

Oh, the power of God that is there and available for us. If we only knew how much the angels have to do with our victory here and how God wants us to have victory all of the time. All the angels that I saw were very specialized and each one had its intended purpose.

I saw that there were multitudes and multitudes of angels in another place that were given to us for wisdom. They would go to the Library of Knowledge and get wisdom and bring it to us. Or they would go with a special instruction to bring and cause it to happen down here. I saw that the Holy Spirit is in charge of it all: He leads; He guides; He directs; and He gives instructions to the angels. The angels do not act on their own, only under the auspices of the Lord Jesus and the power of the Holy Spirit. Only the name of Jesus can loose them for us. When we mention the name of Jesus in our prayers, the Holy

105

Spirit immediately goes into action and begins to direct the action and the angels of God to come into play for us.

I saw that each person that is born again doesn't have only one or two angels. There are literally legions of angels that are at the disposal of the Holy Spirit on our behalf. I saw angels that were in charge of the weather and I saw angels that were in charge of protection. Many times in my life God has sent angels to me.

One time while we were driving, I was given a vision of angels mounted on beautiful white horses and they were traveling along with us beside our automobile. I could see them just like in heaven. And I could hear them. We had been praying for protection and my wife was driving. Suddenly my eyes were open and I heard one of the angels say to me, "I can go faster than you can." I thought that was strange and I told my wife. She said she was thinking, "I wonder what would happen if I put my foot in it." Angels were listening. It is important that we as the children of God keep our thinking right, our words right, and that we allow God to go into action for us.

I saw millions and millions of angels for

every purpose that God has intended in heaven. But I was not allowed to see all of them and none told me their names—I didn't need to know them. Nor would they speak to me unless it was the perfect will of God for them to do so. They are totally obedient to God. There is only one name that we must deal with: our Lord Jesus.

Any time Jesus was near, the angels would stand at attention and look at Him with the most adoration. They would fall at His feet if He wanted to speak to them. They were actually there to serve us as children of God and to serve God in whatever capacity He desired. They were energized to do that. They were empowered to do anything that He wanted them to do.

I knew there were other areas of heaven where I could not go and there were other classes of angels that I was not allowed to see—different types. I was not allowed to know anything about them. But I do know that some of the angels took the form of people and came to earth. Scripture tells us that we have entertained angels unaware. Certainly, we all have heard stories. I saw that they actually came from heaven to do the purpose that God intended.

Hebrews 13:2

*Be not forgetful to entertain strangers:
for thereby some have entertained
angels unawares.* [KJV]

SEVENTEEN
Fields of heaven

I was taken to an area where I looked down upon millions and millions and millions of acres under cultivation. There are huge fields of grain in heaven that are constantly moving in the breeze. They are a supernatural supply for others of different kinds. There is a heavenly harvest that is prophetic.

At one time in my grandfather's life He had some land that he had set aside to pay tithes. He used it when he didn't have cash. He used the income from that land to pay tithes to his church to support it. A drought came. Corn wouldn't grow. Beans wouldn't grow. But he planted this land in wheat because he determined that wheat would grow in pretty dry circumstances. That year of drought, the "tithe" land produced stalks of wheat that were seven feet tall. The people in the area saw and could not describe what had happened except it was the Hand of God. Some said it was a species of wheat they had never seen. That field, by itself, filled the local grain elevator. That is the wheat I saw in heaven.

I saw thousands and thousands of trees filled with fruit. Multitudes of people were coming and picking fruit; taking it away in baskets. They took it to their homes in heaven.

Heaven has animals.

Revelation tells us the Lord returns riding a white horse. I have often wondered about that. What would a white horse from heaven actually look like?

I was taken to an area where there were horse-like creatures. They were supernatural. Some of them had wings. Some had other supernatural abilities that we don't have. They could walk on the air if they needed to.

I saw chariots. Tens of thousands of chariots and beautiful horses to pull them. The horses were white, all white. Every horse I saw was white. They had red hoofs: fiery, crimson, red hoofs. And huge nostrils. They were about 10 to 15 times the biggest horses I have ever seen and were all muscle—no fat. There was no horse by-product to clean up and I don't think they ever ate. They were there for a specific purpose. Some of it had to do with the rapture of the church. Elijah was taken up in a fiery chariot. And I can tell you there was a chariot there that was the Lord's. It was bigger and nicer than the rest and pulled by the most awesome steed.

There were other supernatural animals. I saw a beast that had the body of a giant bull, the neck of a camel and the head of a horse. And I saw an angel sitting on it. I was not told its purpose.

Heaven appears to be a planet millions of times the size of earth. Things are tangible, but not physical.

There are places of heaven no one will ever see. There are continents, fresh water oceans and seas. The seas are large bodies of water surrounded by land but open to the oceans.

There are buildings in heaven that people will never be in.

Conveyances are on the oceans and seas just as they are in the air. Some are very large. Some are hand-carved with biblical sayings carved in them. They seem to exist so people can sit and enjoy each other's companionship. Some are guided by angels.

Land conveyances travel on golden roads. Boat conveyances are on water and the four major rivers. And there are the air conveyances. In them, angels minister blessing to the people just traveling together.

Heaven has huge great factories, but no stacks, no power plants—yet there are common chandeliers all over.

There is a bank in heaven. Our bank. This is how it works. Every time you give anything, it is recorded in heaven. Angels go to a doorway with a slip. They receive golden coins and bring them to earth. The coins are changed to what we need on earth. These are supernatural finances.

EIGHTEEN
Castle of dreams

My angel companion to my right said, "I have brought you here to observe this portion of heaven." He said no more and he wasn't going to. The angel on the left who said very little bowed his head in deep respect and adoration and began to praise the Lord. I fell silent. I just wanted to do the same thing.

Immediately in front of me was the largest castle I could ever imagine. It was suspended in the air many thousands of feet above ground. There were mountains all around and it was the most beautiful castle imaginable. And it was totally crystal clear. You could see right through it.

From the outside, you could not see any people and yet on the inside, there were thousands. The castle was miles high and miles in all directions and when I went through the massive gates, then I saw all the people—it was full of people.

Inside there were great rooms of books. And thousands of angels were tending the books. The people seemed to be heavenly beings that took care of the business of the castle.

There were three Diadem trees growing in the courtyard. They were smaller than the ones I first saw, but each was just as splendid. The angel said, "Remember this," and we were gone.

There is a meaning for the castle. I didn't know until later what it was about. Later, the Lord took me aside and talked to me. He said, "Remember the crystal castle in the sky? This is the place where the hopes and the dreams of my people are kept and fulfilled; from this point." That is where God keeps those hopes and dreams that He wants to fulfill in our lives.

While I was there, I knew the name of the castle, but it was wiped from my mind. All I know is that there is a place where the hopes and dreams that God gives us are stored for us. The angels became very respectful in the presence of the hopes and dreams God has for us. They bowed low.

"Now, it is time for your appointment before

the Throne." They bowed low at the very thought. Suddenly, they simultaneously stood tall, erect, and at attention. The angel spoke to me, "Your time has come to go to the Throne."

Sigmund

NINETEEN
Throne of God

Instantly, we were there.

From the moment I got here, I just knew everything in heaven flowed into and out of the Throne of God. It pulsed like a dynamo. Everything is drawn to the Throne. Everything cycles around the Throne of God.

The Throne Building was huge—beyond my ability to understand. It is the biggest building in heaven. It was several hundred miles wide and at least 50 miles tall. And it had a domed roof. There were living statues with flames coming out of them. And there were columns 30-35 feet across.

There were thousands of steps going up to it. The exact number I don't know, but I do know that each step was significant and prophetic.

As we began to go up the stairway, there were tens of thousands or millions of people going into the Throne and coming out. They were worshiping and praising God. One said, "He is all I thought He was and much more." I heard someone else say, "I just want to go back so bad." They were answered with, "When God's time is right, you will be back here."

A thousand steps up—every step had a purpose. The closer I got, the more magnificent everything became. Proximity causes physical things to become more and more splendid.

Something was done to me to be able to withstand the presence of God.

The entry area or gateway had columns. The number of the columns was also prophetic. They were huge and I have no idea how many there were.

There were more columns that looked like a thousand feet across and tremendously tall. They were in the doorway leading into the Throne.

Suddenly we were through the columns. There were millions multiplied by millions of people prostrate on their faces towards the Throne of God. The Throne faces every direction at the same time and was 25 miles tall. From any part of heaven, you can see the Throne of God.

The Throne was off in the distance quite far away, but even at this distance, the angels were very contrite and in deep repose. They were in awe and were prostrating themselves. I found myself on my face before God. All I wanted to do was worship and praise Him.

The Throne was made out of some heavenly material and it was crystal clear. Yet, it was some type of stone that was gold and ivory and silver and precious gems and jewels—all sparkling. It gave off what looked like light rays that came out of the material it was made of. And great waves of glory swept through it: liquid fire going through the building material. The building gave off rays of glory.

Something had happened to my eyes and I was able to look at the things of God or else they would have been too brilliant for my natural eyes.

From this distance I could tell that there was a being on the Throne. But He was covered with a cloud of glory that radiated

119

from Him: an all consuming, enfolding fire, that was the glory of God Himself. He dwelt in a fire of glory.

The fire must have been the same thing Moses saw in the burning bush. Whatever it is, it surrounded the being on the Throne. I could tell that there was a being in the fire and I could tell there was a Throne and I could tell He was looking at me.

I felt like a grain of sand on the sea shore. I wanted to crawl under people. I was actually in the presence of Almighty God.

Such reverential fear fell upon me—not a dread—but a reverential fear of actually being in the presence of Almighty God. Unbelievable. That fear fell on everybody as they got closer and closer to the Throne.

I could not stand. Nobody could.

Thousand upon thousands of people were going in and out. There were millions of people around the Throne worshiping God. Some were in deep contrition. Some were standing. But most were lying on their face before God thanking Him for what He had done for them.

Inside were seven big pillars. And then there were nine pillars of a substance near to God. I believe they are the Gifts of the Spirit.

There is an inner court surrounded by pillars. And a pavement area with millions of people laying prostrate—some on their backs—all facing the Throne. The pavement was like the pavement Jesus stood on with 100,000 acres of inlaid jewels.

The Temple had a foundation, but I was not allowed to know more.

I got closer to the Throne. There was an area with a railing. Actually, there were three levels of railings. Humans are not allowed beyond them. The railings are made out of gold and some other kind of material that radiated the Glory of God and may be the same as the Glory of God. Angels stood at the railings.

Around the area were stones that were on fire; living stones shaped like a potato gave off blue and amber Shekinah glory. They were from the altar of God and roughly two feet in diameter. They looked like they were coals from the altar of God and on each one of them was a name.

My name was on one of these coals before the altar of God. Again, I was instantly on my face before God. All I wanted to do for all eternity was give glory, honor, and praise to God. The feeling is multiplied millions of times over, stronger and stronger, but it is the same as now when I am in deep prayer and seeking God. You don't want to come out.

While I was in the glory cloud, I was not allowed to look very far. I tried to lift my head but something would push it down. Not as if I could see God—I couldn't—but I could tell there was a being on the Throne.

I never saw God. I was not allowed to see God. Except His toe: like the size of Tennessee. And His foot: like the size of the United States. These are just my words to try and describe what is indescribable.

The Word tells us that the earth is His foot stool. I see how the world could be His foot stool.

Isaiah 66:1
This is what the LORD says:
"Heaven is my throne,
and the earth is my footstool. [NIV]

The glory He was clothed with radiated out from Him and it sounded like a million, million, million, and millions of dynamos of current and power surging out from Him.

Woosh.

Woosh.

Just surge upon surge of power. I just knew these surges of power were answers to someone's prayer. God answers prayer from His glory.

Then there was a raised area beyond this magnificence. There were beings on the throne and flames went in and out. Around the Throne were winged creatures that flew around and around saying, "Holy, holy, Lord God Almighty." I actually saw them doing just that, but I can't describe them. I know that every time they went around the Throne, they saw a different aspect of God. He was totally revealed to them.

Four rivers came out of the Throne. They came out of the glory cloud and ran over the coals but the water did not extinguish the coals—no hissing—they could not be put out. And the water wouldn't. The rivers came out as one from the Throne across the pavement and then to the area prepared for them. Four distinct flowings of water. The small streams were about a half mile wide. They flow through heaven and are bottomless. One of the rivers was the flow of the mercy and grace of God.

All the time I saw memorials to the glory of God for what is done. I saw Jesus talking to others and yet He was "always" behind me. There was what looked like a band shell in the Throne of God. Jesus was there. He looked at me and I just had no words—then or now. It seemed important to Him that I noticed Him. Everything in heaven notices Him, but for some reason He wanted me to remember this. I looked on Him and He smiled.

Whew!

There is a scripture that says not to fear them that can destroy the body but fear Him who can destroy the body and soul in hell. That is God alone. He has the power of eternity. I knew that from the being on the Throne.

Matthew 10:28
And fear not them which kill the body,
but are not able to kill the soul:

but rather fear him which is able to destroy
both soul and body in hell. [KJV]

In front of the Throne, I saw a laver basin
filled with the blood of Jesus.

Everything flowed from the Throne. It
flowed out from the Throne: liquid plasma,
waves of glory. The hopes and desires of
everyone that has ever lived flowed into the
Throne. And out of the Throne flowed God's
love and the answer to our prayers. All
were there.

Another thing I noticed, the people that
were in heaven did not necessarily get to see
God right away. Sometimes they had to
wait for a long time. I think they have to be
there for a while to be able to withstand
being in His presence. It is something
about eating the fruit and smelling those
beautiful leaves as you come into the garden
that helps you to withstand the very
presence of God—to keep you from just
melting.

There were waves of liquid love coming out
of God. The fragrance would choke you
here. But it is beautiful beyond belief: the
aroma of God's presence. Sometimes in

125

Revival services here, the heavenly fragrance has been released. We have smelled it many times, but not at the intensity as it was in A Place Called Heaven.

Out of the glory of God I saw a puff of smoke that went by me like a big plane—millions of dynamos. This is my anointing being sent.

I watched the angels who brought prayers. They were given the substance of God sent with an answer. Everything—all answers—are designed out of His glory.

While before the Throne and throughout the portion of heaven I saw, I noticed lots of some racial groups but fewer of others. It is as though some groups as a whole mostly rejected the Gospel.

When it is time to leave, you migrate back to what you are to do. Every person has a God-designed purpose.

I was before the Throne for what I thought was a long time, but suddenly, I was not there. I was glowing with light and could not speak. But I was not alone. All coming from the Throne were about in the same condition and all were giving God the glory.

Unbelievable peace and tranquility.

Indescribable.

Then the angel told me, "You have an appointment with the Lord."

Instantly, I was at a park-like setting going towards something like a gazebo. Going at the speed of thought.

Sigmund

TWENTY
"Sit, I have somewhat to say to you"

I couldn't walk.

I was picked up and carried from the Throne. I heard a voice, "You are destined to an audience with the Master."

Jesus stood on a platform. He was 180-190 pounds with a reddish-brown beard. He had scars on His face and neck and they were open wounds that were not healed. His feet were scarred. He wore a seamless robe of light; engulfed in a glory cloud of light.

There were seats around the gazebo. The Lord turned and His attention was on something else. When He turned, I fell flat on my face. The power of God just knocked me right down.

Somehow, He stood me on my feet. He must have touched me. The angels were also on their faces. He told them something, but I don't remember it.

"Sit, I have somewhat to say to you." There was a golden chair, like wrought iron, but gold.

"When you were a child, I came to you." I was seven. He came down in a golden stairway. And He came again in my youth.

"I have called you as a prophet to the nations. In many ways you have succeeded. In many ways the evil one hindered and overcame you. But fear not, I have overcome him."

"I was there when you were born. I was there when you were four and the evil one tried to destroy you."

I had measles, scarlet fever and other sicknesses. The doctor gave up. My mother was rocking me while my dad was in the field plowing. Suddenly the house filled with smoke like it was on fire, but it didn't smell. My mother cried out, "God, if you spare this boy..." Out of the cloud came two hands that healed me.

"Son, I'm going to take you to the other

place. I want to do more through you. Richard, I need your help. You were never designed to be more than what you are. This is heaven where I want my people to come."

Thousands of people were listening to what He was saying to me. He told me about people in my life or who would be in my life. He told me some very personal and private things about my life. Some of the heart aches and troubles that I would have—the things I was going to go through:

"One is and will not be and one is next to come."

"Beware, the evil one would send you to wrong people."

He told me that the great revivals are about to spring out in His church. And He is going to cause great revivals to come in small places and that I would be here to see this. And He talked to me of many other things.

Holding His hands out flat, He gestures, "All is taken and brought together."

Sigmund

TWENTY-ONE
The other place

Come. My Father wills you to see the other place."

Immediately, I had dread and did not want to go. Jesus looked at me and said, "There is no disobedience in heaven," and I was ready to go. I knew that because I was with Him, I would be perfectly all right.

Jesus picked me up and carried me like a baby. There was no give to His body: hard as steel; all powerful arms; strongest being in the universe.

Instantly, we descended into a grey, nasty stench like a rotting carcass. I buried my face in His gown.

"You will not want to see." And I was scared. I had both arms around Jesus' arm. We descended to a flat area. I was at the gates of total destruction. Everything that heaven is, hell is the opposite.

133

They were gates as big as the gates I saw in heaven. They were a black material. I remember stairs. And there were hideous beings as tall as the angels that guard the gates of heaven. They were grotesque. Some cartoon figures of demons approach how hideous these creatures were. When they saw the Master, they screamed in horror.

And there were flames of punishment. I felt the doom and despair. I heard people crying out. Demons take people and torture them to the same level of pain they are in. People are naked. There was no one there who was not old enough to know what sin was. There were no babies.

Jesus told me to tell people what I saw. "I want you to tell others of this place and warn them that unless they are washed in my blood, unless they are born again, this is where they will spend eternity."

There were demons all around, screaming, screaming, screaming at the very presence of Jesus. They could not stand to be in His presence. They would scream and run in terror.

There were people begging and pleading

with Him to get them out of there. He would not hear them because their judgment was fixed.

I cannot describe everything I saw because it makes me violently ill. I don't want to remember. But I can tell you there is absolute horror.

When you die, you have a spiritual body. The spiritual body that you have has exact properties that your physical body has when you are alive. But, you are a spirit being. Yet, all physical senses are there.

I saw people there that were walking skeletons with flesh of some kind hanging off of them—rotting off of them. Maggots—and the smell was un-breathable.

People are raped. Serpents eat and digest parts of people and the people are restored and it happens again.

Demons tear people apart. I saw people ripped apart. Parts of their bodies were hanging on boulders and rocks and the demons would take the parts and eat them and pass them through. And then the body was whole again for the process to be repeated.

A young girl had hot coals forced in her mouth with demons mocking, "You really thought you were getting by with something."

There were bunches of people in small cages that were on fire. People are put in small burning cages that are dipped in a lake of fire, but the body is not consumed. The bodies are never consumed. They were half skeleton/half beings.

Demons poured liquid fire on people. There were what was like coal pits burning.

People had cancer with all its pain and suffering—forever.

One man had a rotting arm. It took 100 years to rot off. Then it was restored so it could rot off again.

There was a man with part of his head blown off from war. He had to keep looking for the rest of his head.

I saw the Lake of Fire with people in it bobbing around. Every torment you can imagine is multiplied a million times.

There are degrees of punishment in hell.

Those who are punished the greatest, knew the most and didn't do what they should have done. I thought of Hitler and I thought of God's justice.

There is a hole. In the bottom of the hole there are chained demons. When they saw Jesus, they screamed out, "We're coming to get you." Jesus said, "No you won't."

I pleaded, "Please, I don't want any more."

There are pits of hell that are now empty; empty waiting for whole nations.

I saw more women than men in hell. The women scream in horror at each other.

It is dark and there are demons and serpents everywhere. The demons inflict more pain than they are going through themselves.

Isaiah 66:24
"And they will go out and look upon the dead bodies of those who rebelled against me; their worm will not die, nor will their fire be quenched, and they will be loathsome to all mankind."

Then I saw the place reserved for the devil and his angels: flaming, slimy, fire over his head for a thousand years. The Lake of Fire had depths that got worse and worse and worse.

"Son, you have fulfilled what God wanted." We ascended to the platform again.

I asked, "Who am I going to tell?"

Tell others about A Place Called Heaven—and the other place, the place of separation.

He took His hands and turned my face up into His, one hand on either side of my face. He bent my neck upward so I had to look directly into His face. He said, "Don't ever forget how much I love you and what I have done for you. Never forget how much I love those that you are going back to and the place I have prepared for them and how much I love them."

TWENTY-TWO
"You are going back"

Jesus said, "You are going back."

I sighed and Jesus rebuked me. "The will of my Father is never grievous."

"Stand to your feet. You must go back. You will come back to heaven. You will have angelic visits." Then Jesus hugged me.

And suddenly, my body was full of pain. There was a sheet over my face. I could feel my bones knitting together. I was being healed and I heard a voice, "He's been dead all these hours."

I could feel my left wrist where the bone had been protruding—I could feel it popping into place and healing up.

"It is about time to embalm him."

I remember sitting up and saying, "I ain't dead yet."

Someone hollered in the hall, "He's alive. That dead man is alive." I remember a doctor coming in saying, "I pronounced him dead. And he is dead."

But I was sitting up.

Other doctors and nurses came in and I began to tell the story of where I had been and what had happened. People were weeping. Doctors said, "This must be a miracle of God."

Epilogue

Since then I continue to have visitations of the Lord. Since that time God has poured out His Spirit in my life and I have literally seen the dead raised. I continue to see the blind see, the deaf hear, and the lame walk. Every service I am in I see the outpouring of the Holy Spirit and God performing the miraculous.

I tell this story and when I do, we have a great number that want to get right with God. I would. I would want to go to A Place Called Heaven.

I continue to have angelic visitations. But the two angels that escorted me through heaven, I have never seen again—that I know of—but I have had numerous other angelic visitations. And God is much more rich and much more free to me.

I have a depth of God in my life now to where I never knew was possible. It just seems like this type of revelation is more than any man could ever have. This type of experience with God would seem like one out of a hundred or once in a lifetime, but it now happens to me on a daily basis. Every day I hear the audible voice of God in some manner. Every day I get to see the angels of God. And I have seen Jesus on numerous occasions.

In revival meetings, the angels are visible to me. The cloud of glory is visible to me. The sickness and diseases in people's bodies are visible to me. The demons that afflict them are visible to me. The glory that comes upon them when God heals them is also visible to me.

God has truly poured out upon me a prophetic ministry of signs, wonders, and miracles. And I am to tell the story that Jesus is coming soon. He told me before He sent me back that I would come back and when I did, I had to tell His people to get ready—these are the words of the Lord.

He said, "Prepare yourselves and get ready because I am coming back soon at a time when people don't think I am coming back, I am coming back." He is coming after His sons and His daughters and He is coming after His servants; He is coming after all of us that we might go with Him to that place called heaven. Are you ready? Are you really ready? If you aren't, you can be. Simply confess Jesus Christ as your Savior.

Romans 10:8-10

That if you confess with your mouth,
"Jesus is Lord," and believe in your heart
that God raised him from the dead,
you will be saved.
For it is with your heart that you believe
and are justified, and it is with your mouth
that you confess and are saved. [NIV]

Sigmund

Author

Richard Sigmund was born to John William and Ruth Florence (Custer) Sigmund on March 19, 1941, in Des Moines, IA. His Grandfather was praying while he was being born and the Lord told him, "Through him I will answer prayer." Whose prayer? The prayer of his Great Grandfather, a Spirit-filled Jewish Circuit Riding Preacher during the Civil War. Sometimes God has to skip a generation for anointing.

Seven years later after the Lord appeared to Richard, he started preaching in a country Methodist church in Iowa. His Grandfather who knew Jack Coe told the Evangelist about this child preacher. Rev. Coe brought Richard to Omaha in 1949 to preach. While the boy who became known as "Little Richard" preached, the anointing came upon him. He saw angels while he preached.

When Richard became about nine years old, A.A. Allen had this child preacher present the anointed Gospel ahead of his meetings. Sometimes Richard would come a day or two early to prepare the people for the ministry of the world-renown Evangelist and miracle-worker. "Little Richard" gathered a crowd; he was a "draw." He was with A.A. Allen about 10 years through his teenage years. His Grandfather acted as his manager and ensured tutors were available for schooling. When at home, he was registered in public schools. Also during that time Richard was with Evangelist Lee Girrard and presented his testimony during William Branham meetings.

Always with independent, non-denominational organizations, Sigmund was most frequently affiliated with Emmanuel Pentecostal Evangelistic Association (EPEA), but most recently is with World Bible Way Fellowship. Meetings have been held with numerous independent churches as well as Pentecostal denominations such as Assemblies of God churches.

He had homes in Des Moines and then Miracle Valley, AZ, with the A.A. Allen community. In his early twenties, Richard made some poor decisions. By this time—age 23—he had his own successful ministry in Phoenix, AZ, but because of and connected with those poor decisions, lost it. Picking up the pieces, he continued with tent meetings with considerable success with the Navajo in northern Arizona and other revival meetings around the country. In 1974, he was ministering at a small church in Bartlesville when he was declared dead for eight hours after a traffic accident.

Richard had television programs. He had regular radio broadcasts. His ministries were called "Voice of Healing," and "Echoes of Calvary." Today it is "Cleft of the Rock Ministries" out of Unionville, MO. He has produced 23 books which are all now out of print. He has numerous teaching audio tapes and a video set on "A Place Called Heaven."

Richard has been in meetings with Kathryn Kuhlman (wearing a leisure suit), Oral Roberts, and has been interviewed by Pat Robertson. He has ministered in England, Perth, and when in South Africa, he followed David Nunn and Maurice Cerrullo in a special series of meetings. Rex Humbard encouraged him to tell his story of "A Place Called Heaven."

In the early 90s, he met his wife Priscilla and they moved to Texas in about 1993. While there, L.D. Kramer, a pioneer television evangelist (probably the first) came to his door. Kramer had been to some of Richard's meetings and knew of him. And another healing evangelist, Loretta Blasingame also knew of Richard and wanted to meet him. L.D. arranged the meeting and was also a key player in introducing Richard to World Bible Way Fellowship.

In about 1998, Richard and Priscilla felt led of the Lord to move north to Missouri. Priscilla was originally from Iowa, the same as Richard. Since then, their ministry has been centered from there.

Richard and Priscilla are available for ministry and may be contacted at:

Cleft of the Rock Ministries
P.O. Box 241
Unionville, MO 63565

Phone: 660-947-7581
Email: siggie@nemr.net

Index

153

Sigmund

Contact Information

Dr. Richard Sigmund
P.O. Box 177
Maxwell, IA 50161

Cleft of the Rock Ministries
Telephone: (515) 387-1230
Email: theheavenbook@aol.com

A Place Called Heaven
Book Order Form

If you wish to purchase additional copies of this book, please contact us at the address below, by phone, or email.

Discounts available for volume orders

Name _____

Address _____

_____

Number of books desired _____

Number of CD's desired _____

Cleft of the Rock Ministries
P.O Box 177
Maxwell, IA
50161
515-387-1230
theheavenbook@aol.com